Y0-DWL-161

Halloween Night

written by Dandi
illustrated by Lynne Schwaner

Something strange is going on.

Excitement's in the air.

Do you know what night this is?

The clues are everywhere.

Dogs are howling at the moon.

Every note is out of tune.

Bats stop hanging upside down,
Spread their wings and fly to town.

Ghoulish ghouls can hardly wait!

Vampires wake to celebrate.

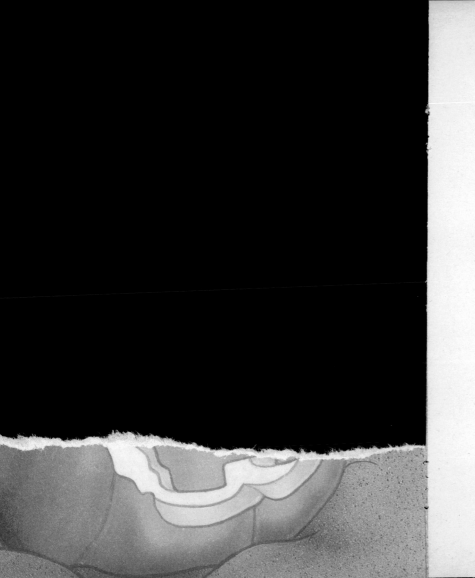

Mummies leave their mummy tombs.

Witches fly on witches' brooms.

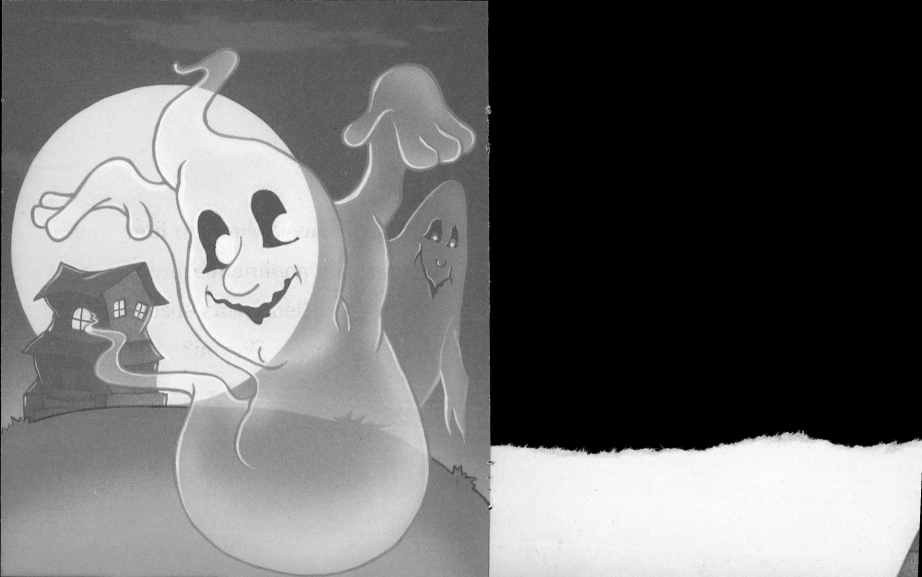

Haunted houses come to life,

Ghosts and goblins too.

What's it called – this special night?

They all know. Do you?

Mummies leave their mummy tombs.

Witches fly on witches' brooms.

On this special night of nights
Kids, both big and small,
Put on costumes. They can dress
As anything at all.

Sister is a dancer,
Brother is a knight.
Cousin wears a monster mask,
Makes him look a fright!

Children go from house to house
Yelling, "Trick or Treat!"
Fill their bags with lots of candy,
More than they can eat!

Have you added up the clues
About what night I mean?

Do you know
What night this is?

It must be...